INSPIRING STORIES
FOR CURIOUS BOYS

TRUE MOTIVATIONAL TALES TO BUILD SELF-CONFIDENCE, COURAGE, AND KINDNESS FOR YOUNG READERS

CHRIS MUNOZ

ISBN 978-1-965031-01-8

2

TABLE OF CONTENTS

INTRODUCTION

Inspiration. That warm soaring of the heart. The desire to do more, be better, jump out of bed, and just go for it. The fidgety hands, the pulsing energy coursing through your limbs. There's nothing quite like it!

Here's the thing though—it's not always easy to feel super excited every day. Sometimes, we find ourselves in a routine where days can start to feel a bit too similar, like rewatching the same episode of a show over and over aaand over again.

We often don't look forward to tomorrow, thinking our daily tasks are unimportant and tedious, our thoughts uninteresting, our activities not very worth doing.

We'd rather turn on some form of entertainment and enjoy it in a stupor. We're not looking for opportunities to seize. We're coasting. Sadly, it's quite easy to live life in this state.

But if you're looking to escape that gray-colored, dullness-laden land, if you're looking for excitement and discovery, the best place to go is to stories of great people.

If you want to live an exciting life, and have an impact, it's a smart idea to look at the examples of those who've impacted the world before you.

Greatness comes in all shapes and sizes, and all types of gifts bring it about. The stories in this book look into the lives of incredibly different men from very different backgrounds. From athlete to astronaut, physician to film-maker, sprinter to skateboarder, stories of all kinds are found here. Each one holds its own unique nuggets of inspiration.

Some of the men in these stories find their adventures in physical challenges. Action, competition, excitement. If these are your preference, rest assured, you won't be bored.

Some of these men find their adventures in the world of ideas. Figuring out difficult problems, exploring the worlds of science and mathematics, of public policy and literature. If you like to explore with your mind, you'll find kindred spirits here.

What ties them all together, though, is that these men worked to make the world a better place. They explored realms no one else had in order to pass on their knowledge to future generations. They worked to make political and social change to improve life for those around them. They pushed their physical limitations beyond what mankind had ever formerly achieved to show the world that humanity is beautiful and amazing and worth fighting for.

So, if you're ready to learn and be entertained, to gain knowledge and motivation all in one go, keep reading. You'll find rich stories meant to do nothing more than inspire you to dream big, to work hard, to become the best person you can be. They'll get you excited so you can start working on your own amazing story.

Dwayne swaggered down the hallway, laughing with his buddies as his classmates scurried out of the way. Bad news. That was his reputation, and he intended to keep it. Anyone who crossed him would regret it. He was no stranger to fighting or breaking rules. Everyone would be happier if they stayed out of his way.

"I'll catch you in class, guys," he said, stepping aside and into a restroom. It was a teachers' toilet, but what did Dwayne care? What were they going to do? Suspend him again?

When he was washing his hands, one of the teachers walked in. Mr. Cwik.

"Hey, you can't be in here," he said.

Dwayne looked over his shoulder at him. "Okay. I'll leave when I'm done." He continued to wash his hands.

Mr. Cwik stared at him, clearly fuming at the disrespect. Dwayne finished and left, smirking as he considered the rage on the teacher's face. No one dared to cross him.

But later that night, that expression haunted his thoughts. As his mother served dinner and talked about how she hoped things were going better at school. As he lay in bed, staring up at the ceiling, he thought of what it was like to be a teacher. How hard it must be to have to teach a bunch of mouthy kids. It was a rough job. And he was making it rougher for no reason.

So, the next day at school, when he saw Mr. Cwik in the hallway, Dwayne stopped him.

"I just want to apologize for how I acted yesterday. And I'm sorry." Dwayne held out his hand for the teacher to shake.

The teacher stared at his hand, then at him, then back at his hand. He took the hand and shook it hard, not letting go.

"I appreciate that, son. Now I've got something to ask you. Have you ever thought about playing football?"

Dwayne laughed. "Me? On the team?"

"Why not?" Mr. Cwik didn't smile. "You've got the build for it, and you clearly already work out to keep yourself in that kinda shape."

Dwayne shrugged. "Yeah, I work out. So what?"

"You might as well put all that muscle to use. Give it a try. Practice is after school today at 3:30. Be there, all right?"

Dwayne shrugged again. "Whatever."

But after school that day, he was on the football field. He had no idea that joining that team would change his life forever.

Dwayne Johnson, known by many as "the Rock," is most known for his prominence as a professional wrestler and now as an actor. But Dwayne didn't see any of that in his future as a kid. In fact, as a kid, he didn't think much about his future at all.

Johnson was the son of wrestler Rocky Johnson, and his mom's dad, Peter Maivia, was a wrestler too. When his parents divorced in his early teen years, he and his mother struggled financially, getting evicted from their home. Dwayne felt helpless to do anything to make his or his mother's life better, and he started working out to feel more in control.

In these troubled times, Johnson also got mixed up with the wrong crowd. As he said, "I was getting in trouble; I was doing a lot of things I shouldn't have been doing, getting arrested. That started happening when I was 13 years old." Dwayne went to four high schools because he kept getting expelled for fighting. He was part of a gang and got mixed up in check fraud and small thefts. No one would have expected success for this kid.

But everything changed when he apologized to one of his teachers for disrespecting him in a teachers' bathroom. The teacher was head football coach Jody Cwik. He invited Johnson to join the team, impacting the Rock's life forever. Dwayne said, "My grades got better, and I started getting recruited from every college across the country. My thought process started to change. That's when I started thinking about goals and what I wanted to accomplish."

Though Johnson's dreams of becoming an NFL star never came to fruition, he is still grateful to Coach Cwik for believing in him. Johnson came to see that he could pursue worthy goals and find success regardless of past mistakes. He could move on and become whoever he wanted to be.

Now Johnson is considered one of the greatest professional wrestlers of all time. He's a successful actor and businessman. He was voted twice by Time to be one of the world's most influential people.

But there was a time when Dwayne didn't think he was going anywhere. He didn't have dreams or aspirations. He didn't think about the future. When a kind teacher showed him that he could do better than drift through life doing whatever was easy, he stopped thinking about who he was and started thinking about who he could be.

Now when he tells others how to be successful, he says, "Don't be afraid to be ambitious about your goals. Hard work never stops. Neither should your dreams." Johnson had a coach who taught him to dream. Now his dreams are endless.

Are there obstacles in your life that make you think you can't be successful? What do you want to do with your life? Though life can be crazy, make sure you dream about your future. Dream about it and work toward it, and you will become great!

FAME THROUGH SOMEONE ELSE'S VOICE

Benjamin plodded into the newspaper office and hung his newspaper bag on a hook by the door.

"Well, I sold them all today, James."

"Hmmm," said Benjamin's older brother, not looking up from the paper he was scribbling all over with a red-inked pen.

"That's the third day in a row. I'm becoming quite the salesman for you. You ought to up my pay to, I don't know, more than nothing. Not everyone would go to all the trouble to make sure he sold every single copy of The New-England Courant."

"Hmmm," James repeated.

Benjamin sighed and wandered up to the small room where he slept above the printing press. He sat at his desk and looked over the papers he had been working on into the wee hours of this morning. He picked up his pen, dipped it in the ink, and continued. The 16-year-old forgot everything around him as he poured his thoughts onto the page. What he was writing was good. He knew it. Just as good as the silly things James' friends wrote. And he had no problem publishing them.

The boy nodded to himself as he stabbed the last period onto the paper. It was good. He had to show it to James.

He made his way back down to the printing room, clutching the precious paper in his hand. His brother still sat with his red pen, giving what appeared to be a bloody death to the paper in front of him.

"Excuse me, James."

"Ben, I'm busy. I've got enough to worry about without you bothering me. Go talk to Ann about whatever it is that you want."

"Will you please just read this?" Benjamin's voice was pleading. He held out his paper.

James looked at the paper and raised his eyebrows.

Words poured out of Benjamin, thick and fast. "Please, I really think it would be perfect for the Courant. Not even early on, I'm not asking for that. Just a small spot on page 5. You could fit it in between Donaldson and Isaac's essays. It's really quite short. And I can typeset the whole thing myself."

James didn't reach for the paper. "Ben, I've had enough of this nonsense. You're 16 years old. You're a child. You're not ready to have your words printed in a newspaper, and I won't even consider it until you're of age. No more. If you bother me again with your childish trash, I'll give you a good thrashing. Do I make myself clear?"

Benjamin glared at his brother. He crumpled up the paper and threw it into the hearth where it quickly caught the blaze. "Perfectly," he said icily. He stalked from the office.

He was seething. James didn't know anything about it. 16 years old indeed. As if there weren't illiterate adults lining the streets they walked. As if age were the same thing as wisdom. As if young people couldn't have good ideas too. He would show him. He would show James and everyone else that he, a 16-year-old, had ideas worth hearing.

An idea stopped him, and Benjamin stopped walking. Of course! That was it! He sprinted back to the office, pounded up the stairs to his room, and began writing again.

Benjamin entered the shop to see his brother laughing over a sheet of paper with his friend, Tom Wilkins.

"It's really got the right tone for the Courant, hasn't it?" James asked his friend.

"Precisely!" Tom said. "Satirical, witty."

"And it's a good length. It'll fit nicely on the third page. And we're to receive a letter every two weeks, so it can be a regular piece for a awhile." James laughed again. "The writer calls herself 'Silence' - ha! Silence indeed, writing for a newspaper! How ironic." He laughed again, wiping his eyes.

"What are you all going on about," asked Benjamin, hanging up his bag and assuming an utterly innocent tone.

James' smile vanished. "Nothing you need to worry about Ben. I'm done with you for today. You can head home to Ann."

"Oh, James," said Tom, ruffling Benjamin's hair in a way he loathed, "don't be so ill-mannered with your little brother. Let him join the fun. Listen to this, Benny. Someone submitted this letter yesterday. It goes like this, 'Sir, It may be improper...'"

Tom read the whole letter aloud. Benjamin laughed at all the right places.

"Well, that's great stuff," he said at the end.

James scoffed. "As if your opinion matters. Head home to Ann."

Benjamin bowed. "Of course. As always, big brother, I am at your service." He hid his smile as he slipped out the door.

Benjamin Franklin was an inventor, a statesman, a diplomat, a publisher, a philosopher, and a writer. He was the man sent to Paris to negotiate the Treaty of Paris that ended the Revolutionary War. He was one of the founding fathers, the first postmaster general, and now has his picture on the $100 bill.

Franklin didn't have an easy start in life though. He was born into a family of 17 children, and his formal education ended when he was 10 years old. At 12, he was made an apprentice to his older brother, James. This apprenticeship was not a happy one. Benjamin, in his autobiography, said that James often beat him and didn't give him any kinder treatment for being his younger brother. James also refused to let Benjamin write anything for the paper.

Benjamin decided he'd get his work in the paper by putting it under a false name. He began writing letters under the name Silence Dogood, pretending to be an elderly woman. The letters were humorous, making fun of various social norms at the time. The letters became very popular and several men sent letters to the Courant proposing marriage to Mrs. Dogood. Eventually, James found out that Benjamin wrote the letters and was angry.

Benjamin, at 17, ran away from his apprenticeship to find work in Philadelphia. He worked there for a year before becoming a journeyman printer in London. A few years after that, he purchased The Pennsylvania Gazette. Benjamin became quite wealthy through this and his publication Poor Richard's Almanac. He was able to dedicate his life to his inventions and statesmanship.

Benjamin refused to be told that he wasn't old enough or smart enough to make a difference. He didn't give up. He thought things through, and he found a way to have his voice heard. Even if he had to pretend it was someone else's voice.

Sometimes it's hard to keep trying when people tell us we're not ready yet or we're not good enough, but the important thing is to persevere. Even if some people don't think we can do it, we've got to keep on trying. How can you practice not giving up in your life?

IT DOESN'T MATTER WHAT
THEY THINK

The bat cracked, and Tony saw the ball soaring toward him. He tried to follow it, and held up his glove. He missed. The ball dropped to the ground. He scrambled to grab it and throw it in, but the damage was done. Two runners scored before the ball made it back to the pitcher. He glared at Tony before turning back toward the plate to deal with the next batter. Tony sighed.

The inning ended, and the game was over. They had lost 7-6. Tony headed into the dugout, his head hanging, avoiding eye contact with everyone.

"Nice going, Tony," said the shortstop, smacking him in the back of the head. "We woulda won if it wasn't for you."

"Yeah Tony, next time why don't you take a little longer to throw the ball in? Then they can get three runs instead of two."

Tony didn't respond. He plodded out of the dugout toward home.

"Don't bother to show up next time, Tony!" the second-baseman called after him. "The other teams are the only ones who'll miss you!"

Tony kicked the sidewalk with every step on the way home. Stupid, stupid, stupid. Why couldn't he get any of it right? He'd been trying for so long. Wouldn't he ever get better at baseball?

When he got home, his friend, Freddy, was waiting for him, leaning on the fence, his skateboard next to him. "Hey Tony, why the long face?"

"Nothing. Just a stupid baseball game."

Freddy shivered. "Baseball. I don't know why you bother hanging out with those guys. They're jerks to you anyway."

Tony shrugged.

Freddy picked up his board. "You wanna skate?"

Tony nodded. He dropped his backpack in the kitchen and grabbed his board from his room. They rode down the street together. Tony began to circle around at the normal spot, but Freddy grabbed his arm and pulled him forward.

"Not this time, Tony. We're going to the park."

Tony had never been to a skate park before. He watched as older boys sped back and forth in giant bowls, jetting up into the air on either side.

Flying, he thought. It's like they're literally flying.

"You wanna try?" Freddy asked.

"Yeah," Tony said in a whisper.

Tony began to haunt the skate park after that day. He rode his board everywhere. He used all his time after school to practice. Soon he was being bullied for carrying his skateboard around.

"Surfboards don't have wheels, dork," someone said as he walked down the hall.

"You know, dude," said Freddy, "I'm glad you love skating, but you really shouldn't carry your board around school. It's just asking for harassment."

"You're right," said Tony. "I'll keep it in the bushes outside starting tomorrow."

Freddy grinned. "You're obsessed, man."

Tony looked at the other kids passing them in the hall, pointing at his board and laughing. "You know what?" he told Freddy. "It doesn't matter what they think. I feel bad for them. They don't know what they're missing. They just don't know how cool skateboarding is."

"You show 'em, Tony." Freddy ducked into his class.

Tony continued down the hall, ignoring the rude looks and words, dreaming of the next time he'd get to fly.

Tony Hawk is regarded by many as the greatest skateboarder of all time.

He won the world championship 11 years in a row, won 6 gold medals in a row at the X-Games, and was the first boarder to complete and land a trick called the 900, which many skateboarding experts believed to be impossible to do at the time.

Hawk said he skateboarded for the first time when he was 10 on his brother's board. He rode it down an alley, asking his brother, "How do you turn this thing around?" When he got there, he just got off the board and turned it around by hand.

However, Tony really got into the sport after visiting a skate park with some friends. He'd tried playing other team sports with little success. He didn't feel like he was improving even though he kept practicing. This wasn't the case with boarding. As Hawk said, "It was incremental, almost too small to measure, but I knew each time I was improving and I couldn't say that about any of the other sports I was doing."

The hobby was very unpopular at the time, having mostly an underground following. He started hiding his board in the bushes outside his school, even though he was already a pro athlete with sponsors. He'd been a victim of bullies before, and draggin a skateboard around became yet another reason for other kids to pick on him.

But Hawk didn't let the bullying stop him. When talking about the bullying he suffered for skating, Hawk said, "that gave me the reason to try harder and make it more legitimate. I felt like I had something that they didn't really understand and I liked that. I liked that it set me apart and I didn't care what they thought."

By the age of 14, Hawk was skating professionally, sponsored by the Powell-Peralta skateboard company. By the age of 17, he'd earned enough to buy his own house. He now owns a video game franchise and a few clothing labels that keep his bank account happy. Though he's retired from competing, Hawk says he'll continue to skate until he's physically unable.

Though Tony was made fun of and told he couldn't make it in the world of skateboarding, he kept going. He knew what he loved, and he didn't care what other people thought about it. He thought of himself as "set apart," not as an oddball. He kept practicing and made something great of himself.

Sometimes other people make fun of our interests and passions. Have you ever been made fun of for something you like to do? Do you ever try to hide things you enjoy to "fit in" with others?

How could you, like Tony, practice not caring what other people think?

How could you practice perseverance in your own life?

NOT A NICE, SAFE JOB

"So, they're saying they hope the launch will happen before the end of summer?" said Buzz, standing at his friend's office door.

"That's the word that's been going around," Neil said, leaning back in his chair. "But who knows. You know they'll call this off for the tiniest thing going wrong." He looked at his watch. "Ope, time to head out."

"You're going home this early in the day? We just had lunch."

"No, they've got me scheduled to take up the old flying bedstead again."

Buzz grinned. "Try to make it down in one piece."

"That's the idea." Neil stood and headed down the hall.

"Hey, look on the bright side," Buzz called after him.

Neil turned back to look at him. "What's that?"

"Maybe the spacecraft will be easier to handle than the LLRV."

Neil laughed. "Or maybe it'll be harder."

Buzz grimaced, and the men headed their separate ways.

30 minutes later, Neil had his gear on and was climbing into the Lunar Landing Research Vehicle (LLRV). He closed the hatch after him.

Most people wouldn't have identified it as a space shuttle. It looked more like someone had welded together a few small electrical towers and glued a box in the middle. A normal person looking at it would have found it hard to believe that it could fly.

This was the aircraft which was supposed to prepare Neil to land on the moon, and it was frightening. The machine was difficult to handle, and, in space, everything was about precision. One small mistake, and, well, he didn't want to think about it.

The LLRV rose from the ground without a hitch, and Neil navigated it around not much more than 50 feet off the ground. He flew it around slowly. Everything was running smoothly. He started to head down to the ground, preparing to land it. This was the most crucial skill he was here to learn after all.

He was 30 feet from the ground, 20, 10, he was about to touch down, and then, without warning, the machine jerked back up. It rose back into the air, ignoring Neil's steering. Then it started to sway one way, then another, rising higher and higher. He had completely lost control.

Neil's mind flew through the options, and he quickly calculated that there was no way he could safely land a spacecraft which he couldn't steer. He ejected himself, soaring from the aircraft, his colorful parachute ballooning up above him. Mere seconds later, the LLRV crashed to the ground and exploded into flame.

Neil watched, the adrenaline pumping through him. He began to descend. Shoot. He hoped the chute would carry him farther from those flames. He managed to land safely at a good distance from the wreck, NASA personnel swarming around him to make sure he was all right.

"Hey, how did it go?" Buzz asked, stopping Neil in the hallway.

"We better hope that space shuttle is easier to handle, not harder," said Neil.

Buzz laughed. "What, did it give you whiplash again?"

"It's smoldering in pieces on the ground outside right now."

His friend stared at him. "You're kidding."

"Try me."

"Are you okay?"

"Yeah, sure. I ejected before it happened." Neil started walking again.

"Where are you going?"

"I've got to file my report."

Buzz grabbed him by the shoulder. "You know, I think you're entitled to an afternoon off when you almost explode."

Neil grinned. "Buzz, I'm all right. I know this isn't a nice, safe job. I like the challenges. We've got to keep working if we want to launch before September." He went into his office and shut the door, going straight to work on his report.

Neil Armstrong was a naval aviator, test pilot, aeronautical engineer, university professor, and, of course, an astronaut. He's most widely known for being the first person to step foot on the moon.

Though many of us have watched video clips of Neil and his friends bouncing around the moon, planting the American flag, and making inspirational quotes and jokes, the journey to get there was not all marshmallows and daisies. It was difficult, dangerous work.

Just two years earlier, during a practice run of space flight for the Apollo space program, three astronauts died of because they couldn't breathe due to a fire and a faulty hatch door. A few months after that, a Russian astronaut, who had actually gone into orbit, died when his spacecraft crash landed in southeastern Russia. Space travel and the preparation for it were dangerous, and Neil Armstrong and all the other astronauts knew that. They knew they might lose their lives. They thought, however, that space exploration was worth it.

Armstrong did in fact eject from a LLRV seconds before it crashed in flames, and he also was reported to have gone back to his desk to finish the day's work afterward. Danger and adventure were part of a day's work for him. They didn't cause him to waver an instant in his desire to complete the lunar landing mission. Challenge wasn't a deterrent for Armstrong. He knew it was just another part of the game.

As Neil himself put it, "I think we're going to the moon because it's in the nature of the human being to face challenges. It's by the nature of his deep inner soul... we're required to do these things just as salmon swim upstream."

Armstrong believed that human beings were made to face challenges, to solve problems, to explore the world and the space in which we exist. He didn't let challenges slow him down, but he faced them and kept on working toward his goals. Because of that, he helped humanity achieve something amazing.

Challenges face us in all aspects of our life. We can see them either as bad or good. To view them as good is to see them as opportunities to learn and grow. What challenges do you face in life?

How could you view them as opportunities to learn?

SUFFERING HELPS US UNDERSTAND

The boy opened the door to the apartment complex and sighed in relief, glad to be out of the hot Hawaiian sun. He was ready to get home. Since he'd moved back from Indonesia to live with his grandparents, school had been...different. Every day, he was ready to get out of there and get home.

The elevator doors opened, and a woman got on. The boy raced to join her before the doors closed. He made it in time and smiled up at the woman.

"Good afternoon, ma'am."

The smile she returned was stiff. "Good afternoon." She stepped off the elevator.

The boy looked at her, puzzled. He'd just seen her get on. And now that he looked at her, he recognized her. She lived down the hall from his grandparents.

"Do you...want to come up?" he asked.

"Oh no," the woman said, still wearing that stiff smile. So the boy rode the elevator to his floor and got out. He saw the elevator descending again. He looked at it for a moment, then ran to his grandparents' apartment, went inside, and stared out the peephole. Sure enough, a minute later, the woman walked past the door in the hall. She just hadn't wanted to ride with him.

The boy headed to his room, sat on his bed, and put his head in his hands. He knew why she had done it. She didn't want to be on the elevator with a black boy. Or half-black. Whatever. His mother, the parent he remembered growing up with, was white. The grandparents he lived with now were white. Half of him was white; he wasn't nearly as dark as his father. But in the eyes of the people here, his chocolate-colored skin and curly raven hair made him black. And for some reason, that didn't seem to be a good thing.

A gentle knock broke into his thoughts. He looked up to see his grandfather peeking in.

"Hey, kiddo."

"Hey, Grandpa."

"Everything okay? We heard you come in."

"I'm...fine."

"Uh huh," his grandpa said, leaning against the doorframe. "And this is what boys do when they're fine? They run to their rooms and hide their faces?"

"I wasn't hiding my face."

His grandfather threw up his hands. "If you don't want to talk about it, that's up to you. I just wanted to make sure you're all right."

The boy sighed. "You wouldn't understand."

"Try me."

He laughed. "How could you understand? You're white!"

The old man nodded. "Yes, I am. Is that what this is about? Have they been teasing you at school?"

"No. Well, kind of."

"What does 'kind of' mean?"

"They made fun of Coretta and me for playing together the other day. They said I was her boyfriend."

His grandfather laughed. "That's just what kids do at this age when boys play with girls. Get a little older, and they'll envy you for it."

The boy didn't smile. "They don't do it when other boys and girls play together. They only made fun of us because Coretta and I are the only black students in the class."

His grandfather stopped smiling. "I see."

"And that's not all!" He explained about the woman on the elevator.

His grandfather joined him on the bed. "This is hard for you," he said.

"No kidding." The boy turned his face toward the ground.

"You know, I'm not going to say that I understand exactly what you're going through. Like you said, I'm white. I've never felt as singled out for my color the way you have. But I can tell you that I've been singled out. I can tell you that I've gone through hard things too. And I've learned that there are two ways you can handle them."

"And what are those?"

"Way number one is to get bitter and angry. You can focus on how unfair it is. You can feel sorry for yourself. Like you seem to be doing right now. But there is another way, Barack."

The boy finally looked up at him. "What's that?"

"You can learn from them. You can remember them when you see other people who are feeling left out. You can be grateful that you know how to help because you do understand. You can let those experiences teach you to care for and help others."

The boy frowned up at his grandfather. "You make it sound easy."

"It's not. But it is worth it, Barack."

He nodded. "Maybe. I guess I'd better do my homework now."

"Well, far be it from me to keep you from that. Hang in there, kid."

"I will, Grandpa."

Barack Obama was the 44th president of the United States. He is known for leading the country through the financial crisis that followed the housing market crash of 2008, for passing healthcare reform, and for ending the U.S. combat missions in Iraq and Afghanistan, among many other accomplishments. He won the Nobel Peace Prize in 2009 "for his extraordinary efforts to strengthen international diplomacy and cooperation between peoples." Oh, and he was the United States's first black president.

Obama rose to prominence surprisingly quickly, but that didn't mean his life was always easy. His father was hardly in his life at all, seeing his son only once after divorcing his mother when Barack was three. He then died when Obama was 21.

Obama attended a private school in Hawaii which was mostly white, and it was around this time that he began to struggle with his racial identity. He got mixed up with a bad crowd in high school and made some bad choices. He credits his success in life to having caring adults in his life who pushed him to be better.

Obama went on to study at Occidental College, Columbia University, Harvard Law School, and University of Chicago Law School. He then went on to become a state senator, then a U.S. Senator, and then, in 2008, the President of the United States.

Though Obama could have become bitter and closed off by his difficulties with racism as a young man, he has instead become a man who focuses on trying to unite his country and the world. Empathy is key to all his accomplishments.

He grew up feeling misunderstood. As an adult, he made it a priority to understand others and consider their perspectives. As he put it, "There is not a liberal America and a conservative America - there is the United States of America. There is not a black America and a white America and Latino America and Asian America - there's the United States of America." He changed from a young man who felt like an outcast to a man who tried to include others and understand them.

The difficulties we face can sometimes make us feel alone and misunderstood. This loneliness, however, gives us the opportunity to reach out to others who are lonely. It can help us understand what they're going through. In what ways have you faced difficulty?

How can it help you care about other people who might have faced the same kind of difficulty?

KEEP TESTING AND LEARNING

"Here we are. Hut 8." said the small man, opening the door for Turing.

"Thank you very much, sir."

He nodded to the man and entered. Several men sat in a circle in the middle of what seemed to be an intense discussion. They stopped talking and stared at Alan.

"Alan Turing at your service," he said. "I've been asked to join you if you'll be good enough to have me."

A tall man with a small mustache stood. "Yes, we were told you'd be coming. I'll catch him up to speed, gents," he said to the group. "You go on." They continued their discussion in hushed tones.

The tall man shook Turing's hand. "The name's Gordon Welchman. Very pleased to meet you, Mr. Turing. I read your dissertation on ordinal-based logical systems. Quite fascinating stuff."

Turing nodded and gave a small smile. "I'm glad you think it's fascinating. I certainly do. So, tell me about this code we're trying to crack."

Welchman drew Turing over to a table where a little metal device sat. "This machine is called Enigma. The Germans use it to encode all the messages they send to their naval fleets. We're able to intercept these messages regularly, but the code is almost impossible to break. It's made even harder by the fact that the Germans change their encryption key every day."

Turing bent down to examine the device. "What a beautiful little piece," he whispered. He looked up at Welchman. "Let's have a look at some of those messages, shall we?"

Welchman smiled and nodded. "Welcome to the team."

"All right, let's run it again!" said Alan, and he flipped the switch. The machine whirred to life, the pieces spinning and clicking away.

"Do you think it'll go this time?" Welchman asked.

Turing shrugged. "If it doesn't, it'll be nothing new."

The clicking stopped and an unhealthy growling sounded from the depths of the contraption. Turing sighed and flipped it off.

"Well, let's see what's wrong this time." He strode to the back of the machine and began opening panels and tinkering.

Welchman laughed. "Don't you ever want a break after a failure."

Turing stuck his head out just long enough to say, "The Germans don't take a break."

Welchman nodded. "Good point." He joined Turning behind the machine.

"I don't see failure as an obstacle," said Turing as he worked his screwdriver. "I see it as a chance to learn."

"Ah, yes," said Welchman. "But I must confess that I hope we haven't much more to learn before it works."

Turing laughed. "I can understand that. But when we're done building it, I hope to be able to keep learning on something else. There's always more, my friend."

"That there is, Alan." And they worked together silently.

Alan Turing is known by many as the father of computer science and artificial intelligence. He was a brilliant mathematician and was recognized as a genius at a young age. He received his doctorate from Princeton, writing several important papers while he was there. He returned to the United Kingdom near the beginning of World War II and was quickly asked to join the code-breaking team at Bletchley Park.

Turing worked with many people at Bletchley, but his main contribution was a machine he made with Gordon Welchman called the bombe. The idea was that a machine could work out Enigma's secret code method and translate the messages much faster than humans could. The machine was completed in 1940.

Once the bombe was up and running, Turing and his team could figure out the messages, but now they had the problem of too many messages to be decoded and not enough machines or people to decode them. Important information was coming in constantly, but they weren't always able to translate it quickly enough for it to be useful. They knew this process was vital to winning the war. In desperation, Turing and his team wrote a letter to Winston Churchill, the Prime Minister of the United Kingdom during World War II, asking for help.

Churchill didn't ignore their request. He sent an urgent message to his chief of staff: "Make sure they have all they want on extreme priority and report to me that this has been done."

They received the help, and soon the decryption work was running full tilt. Historians estimate that this information gave the Allies the chance to end the war two years earlier. Turing and the other people working at Bletchley Park worked together to save millions of lives.

Turing continued working with the Allies to create and break codes throughout the war. When it ended, he studied computers and artificial intelligence, creating the famous Turing Test which was to be used to tell the difference between a machine and a person. Sadly for science and the world, he died of cyanide poisoning, possibly from an experiment gone awry, when he was only 41.

Many of Turing's contributions to computer science were largely unknown during his life. Because he worked on top-secret, code-breaking techniques, much of his work couldn't be made public until many years after his death. However, his legacy is now fully established, with statues of him scattered throughout the United Kingdom, many buildings and schools named after him, and his face printed on the English 50-pound note.

Turing dedicated his life to solving problems. One of the main steps in the process of creating something new is failure. He had to create, test, fail, create, test, and fail. But each time he failed, it was a chance for him to learn. Failure can be very frustrating, but it can also be viewed as an opportunity. The next time you face failure, ask yourself, "What can I learn from this experience?" Chances are, there's always something.

LAZY LIGHTNING BOLT

"We've got some really impressive talent this year," Coach McNeil said, taking a sip as he sat across from his fellow coaches at the coffee bar.

"Do you?" asked another coach with a chuckle. "Well, since we're at the championships, I think we could all say the same."

"I know runners," McNeil said, holding up his finger. "I've coached for years and ran in my own day. But this year, I've got one who could do really well if he learns to put in the work."

The other coach smiled indulgently. "Well, that's what every coach thinks, isn't it? But there's one who's not going to do really well." He chuckled, pointing out the window. A tall, dark boy was sprinting away from the house.

Coach McNeil closed his eyes and stood. "Excuse me," he said.

The coach stomped across the lawn, looking for the boy. Where could he have gone? There weren't many places to hide. Then he saw a shed near the treeline. He headed toward it.

He hammered on the door.

"Usain! Usain, get out here!"

Usain giggled and whispered, "As soon as you find me, Coach."

The door handle jiggled and opened.

"Usain? Where are you?"

Usain covered his mouth, barely able to restrain his laughter.

"This is not funny, Usain! The bus leaves in 40 minutes. Where are you?"

Coach McNeil started searching, looking behind the odds and ends. It was nearly too much for Usain. If Coach didn't find him soon, he'd burst out laughing and give himself away.

Coach pulled aside an old, mildewy tarp. There was Usain, doubled up with laughter, rocking back and forth.

"Usain, get your butt off the floor and back to your room. You're not even dressed."

The boy kept laughing.

"I swear, if you don't grow up and start taking things seriously, you're going to waste all your potential. Just waste it all."

"I-I'm sorry," Usain gasped. "It-it was just too funny." His sides ached, and he couldn't breathe. But he couldn't stop laughing.

"How old are you, 14 or 5? Get off that floor right now. If you have to laugh, be useful while you do it. Get up."

The boy rose to his feet with difficulty, his whole body still shaking. His coach pulled him from the room, and back toward the house. The boy followed obediently, giggles still trickling from him intermittently.

When they reached his room, Coach McNeil held Usain by the shoulders and looked at him. "Listen, boy. You have a gift. I don't think you realize quite how much of a gift it is, but I do. And I'm going to do everything in my power to see that you don't throw it away behaving like an idiot. Remember this, Usain. There's no such thing as a lazy lightning bolt."

"I'm sorry, Coach. I really am. I'll do my best, I promise." The boy held a straight face for a full five seconds. Then another big belly laugh burst from him.

Coach McNeil shook his head. "Just get ready."

Usain nodded and went into his room. Peals of laughter sounded through the door. If only that boy got serious, he'd be amazing. Simply amazing. He'd change the world if he ever wised up.

Usain Bolt, a Jamaican track star considered by many to be the greatest sprinter of all time, didn't always take his sport seriously. As a kid, he loved sports and spent much of his childhood playing football (soccer) and cricket. And, from the get-go, he was fast. In elementary school, he won his school's 100-meter race.

In high school, his cricket coach noticed his speed and pushed him to try track and field.

Bolt's coaches, Pablo McNeil and Dwayne Jarrett, tried to get him to take his running seriously but with limited success. Bolt just wanted to have fun. He wasn't that interested in giving sprinting all his effort and focus.

He loved practical jokes. When he was 14, at the Boys Championships for track in Kingston, his coach saw him sprinting away from their lodgings and had to go hunt him down. Usain pulled a similar prank at the trials for the CARIFTA Games a year later, hiding in the back of a van. He was escorted back to the track by a policeman.

Even with all these silly antics, Bolt was still fast. He won world championships at the youth, junior, and senior levels in track. At 15, he became the youngest-ever world junior gold medalist. He won 4 golds at the CARIFTA Games in 2003 when he was about 16.

He became more disciplined around the age of 18 and started making major improvements. He went to the Olympics in 2008 and got three gold medals, setting world records for the 100- and 200-meter races.

He's now won 8 Olympic medals and 11 world championships. He still holds world records for the 100-meter, 200-meter, and 4x100-meter races.

Bolt is retired now, giving his body a rest after suffering many injuries throughout his career. Though his achievements are incredible, he does wish he hadn't goofed around so much in his younger years.

As he put it, "I wouldn't say it was a regret because everything happens for a reason... but I wish I got serious earlier. Because when I was a junior, if I really took track and field serious, I probably could have won like four Olympics." Though Usain wasn't very disciplined from the beginning, he did accomplish amazing feats when he focused on training and doing his best.

Now he's retired, he participates in many projects. He tries to support Jamaican kids' education and sports efforts.

He was an ambassador for a movement throughout the Caribbean to create sustainable and renewable energy policies. He's also worked with special needs athletes.

The fastest man alive finds these individuals inspiring. Usain says, "For me, it's just all about to show determination, and for me, to see them go out there and work as hard as they do, it also inspires me to know that they have this disability, but they never give up. They want to be great athletes as well."

Perhaps athletes who face such challenges remind Bolt of his former, goofy self. They already have determination and strong work ethics, qualities he had to learn to achieve greatness.

Bolt said, "For me, it's just to leave a legacy to prove to people that anything is possible." He proved that a person could run faster than anyone else had before. He learned to push himself to be his best, and now he wants to help others do the same.

Doing our best is hard work. It's much easier to goof off and take it easy, but our greatest accomplishments tend to happen when we're trying our very hardest. Do you ever tend to be lazy? In what ways? How could you push yourself to work hard and do your best?

DOCTOR CLOWN

Zoila rolled onto her side to face the wall. Coughing and moaning echoed around her. Hospitals were supposed to help people get better, but Zoila felt worse here. Sickness and sadness filled the air.

How could anyone heal in a place like this?

She felt the bandage on her face where her left eye used to be. It was a constant reminder of the explosion that had changed everything. She would be a freak for the rest of her life. People probably wouldn't even want to look at her. And with Mama and Papa gone too, no one would ever really love her again. Her aunt and uncle, who had never liked her, would be her new family. Zoila sighed and rolled over again.

A faint sound of music crept down the corridor of the children's hospital. An upbeat tune filled the room. Zoila sat up. What could that be? She hadn't heard anything so happy the entire time she'd been here. Suddenly, a clown appeared in the doorway. The figure had a curly, green wig, red and white-striped, oversized pants, and a red clown nose. She was playing the violin, dancing down the aisle, and smiling at all the children.

Several other clowns followed her. One handed out little trinkets, smiling and chatting with each child. Another carried a bubble machine, sending happy little orbs bouncing into walls and beds. One popped on Zoila's nose. She couldn't help giggling.

A man with a long gray and green ponytail, glasses, and a tie with flamingos on it pranced up to her bed. He spoke a language that Zoila couldn't understand, but she smiled and nodded anyway. He bent to give her a big hug. Tears came to Zoila's eye. When was the last time someone had hugged her? Had it been Mama?

The man kept chattering, his voice cheerful even though she couldn't understand the words. He pulled a plastic jar from his huge pants pocket and held it out to her. Zoila took it, and he helped her unscrew the lid. Inside was a strange liquid and a long piece of plastic. The man dipped the plastic into the liquid and blew a shimmering bubble. He handed the wand to Zoila. She blew gently, and a perfect bubble formed. A small smile spread across her face as she looked at the man.

"Thank you," she said softly, knowing he wouldn't understand the words but hoping he'd feel her gratitude. He nodded and hugged her again before moving to the next bed, he handed out more little gifts, showed the kids a magic trick, and made silly faces and voices.

For the first time since Zoila had arrived, laughter filled the room. The clowns seemed to have brought sunshine and warmth with their bright clothes and smiles. Zoila kept blowing bubbles, letting the cheerful spheres light up the room with shimmering rainbows.

As the clowns left the hospital, Zoila smiled after them, her heart feeling lighter. She thought of the man with the gray-and-green hair. She thought of the joy he had just brought to her heart. He was not beautiful. In fact, he was quite odd-looking. But he had blessed her with his kindness and care. Perhaps she, even with only one eye, could do something like this for others.

Perhaps she could also bring joy into the world.

She turned her face to the wall again, but despair no longer filled her heart. Instead, it was full of hope and dreams of a future where she brought beauty and life into the world. Where she made people happy. Just as the man with the green and gray hair had made her happy.

Zoila's experience with the kind-hearted clown changed her outlook on life. She found hope in an unexpected place, just as many others have done thanks to a special doctor who believes in the healing power of laughter and kindness.

Hunter Doherty "Patch" Adams is a medical doctor who never practiced medicine in a normal hospital. Nowadays, he travels the world with a group of clowns, bringing joy to people just like he did for Zoila. He visits schools, children's hospitals, crisis centers, and more. As Adams puts it, "The role of a clown and a physician are the same - it's to elevate the possible and to relieve suffering." He sees his clowning as a healing method, more effective, in some ways, than medicine.

Adams, who seems to be endlessly happy, didn't start out that way. When he was a teenager, he felt very sad and lonely. He even had to go to the hospital because he was so unhappy. But while he was there, he had a big idea: he could make the world better by showing love to others. He thought the world was short on love. This was part of why he wanted to leave the world. But instead, he decided to devote his life to loving others and become a doctor who not only gives medicine but also gives love and laughter.

Adams went to medical school at a time when healthcare was very doctor-centered. Physicians didn't spend much time with each patient, and it was normal to try to solve the majority of health problems by throwing medicine at them. The idea was to see the person quickly, diagnose their issue, and prescribe a remedy.

Adams rejected this form of healthcare and began to study holistic health. He did his own research to understand how he could best help his future patients. Adams didn't just want to treat patients, he wanted to love them and help them have the best lives they could.

After earning the title Doctor of Medicine in 1971, Adams began running a free hospital out of a six-bedroom home. He was helped by about 20 of his friends, many of whom were doctors. They ran this hospital for twelve years and cared for hundreds of patients. The hospital focused on knowing each person and creating a community for all to share.

Adams's philosophy of healthcare that cares for the whole person and the community has greatly changed modern healthcare. Medical schools now teach a much more patient-centered, holistic health approach. Mental health has become a major focus in the United States healthcare system when it used to be primarily ignored except in mental health hospitals. Though Adams still hasn't transformed U.S. healthcare as much as he wanted, his ideas have had a lasting impact.

Nowadays, Adams keeps busy by bringing joy and hope to the suffering around the world. All because, at 18 years old, he decided to devote his life to loving others.

Most of us would agree that the world could use a bit more love in it. Dr. Adams shows love by dressing up as a clown and trying to provide holistic care to his patients; but everyone can show love to those around them.

How can you show love to the people in your life?

ALL ABOUT THE DETAILS

"Jimmy! Hey Jimmy, wake up!"

Jimmy groaned and rolled over. "Dude, I only went to bed like three hours ago."

"You've got to look at this! It's happening! Your video is going viral!"

Jimmy sat straight up, sleep washed from his eyes.

"What?"

"It's going viral, man. Look, you've already got 400 views."

His friend sat down next to Jimmy on his mattress, and they both stared at the screen. 400 views. His friend refreshed the page. 402 views.

Jimmy jumped up and started pacing back and forth in the room. "I can't believe this. That video? I mean, it was impossible to get it uploaded with how long it was, but who would think that many people want to watch someone count to 100,000. I need to think about that."

"Dude, you're ridiculous," his friend laughed, refreshing the page again. "410 views now. You've been trying to get this to happen for five years, and now that you've got your first viral video, all you're thinking about is figuring out why?"

Jimmy held out his hands. "Of course. It's not like I only want to make one viral video. I want this to be my job, dude. That means I have to figure out how to consistently make viral videos. I have to figure out what it is that makes people want to watch."

"415 views. Man, you're crazy. You should go back to bed."

Jimmy threw a pillow at his friend. "As if I could now! Now I'm going to be up the rest of the day watching how many views I get and trying to figure out why!" He sat down at his computer.

His friend just laughed. "You're crazy, man. Congratulations."

"Thanks man," Jimmy said distractedly.

Jimmy Donaldson, known by many under the YouTube handle MrBeast, has been all about the details in his YouTube career from the beginning. He started his first channel at 13 years old in 2012 and began studying YouTube algorithms in high school. He was obsessed with how to create videos that would go viral, particularly after Crohn's disease forced him to quit baseball, a sport he loved.

Donaldson went to college for two weeks before dropping out to devote more time to his channel. His mother did not approve and kicked him out of the house, which Donaldson says she did because "she loves me and just wanted me to be successful."

Jimmy's first viral video came out in 2017, a few months after he'd left his mother's home. It was a video in which he counted to 100,000, taking him over 40 hours to record. This experience gave Jimmy an idea. "That's when it kinda clicked – like, 'Oh, if I do interesting things, people will watch,'" he said

Jimmy now has more subscribers than any other individual on YouTube. His videos are highly varied, ranging from titles like "I Spent 7 Days Buried Alive" to "100 Kids Vs 100 Adults for $500,000" to "1,000 Deaf People Hear For The First Time." These videos are known for being incredibly elaborate and entertaining.

Donaldson is estimated to be worth $500 million, but he doesn't consider himself rich. He puts his income back into making better videos. The most recent ones are estimated to cost $1-1.5 million each to make.

MrBeast is also known for his kindness and giving. In 2019, he was part of the Team Trees fundraiser with the goal of raising $20 million for the Arbor Day Foundation, which plants a tree for every dollar donated. They beat their goal.

Jimmy also started the MrBeast Philanthropy channel, which claims that "100% of the profits from my ad revenue, merch sales, and sponsorships will go towards making the world a better place!" This channel hosts videos on topics like building schools, giving away $30 million in free food, and helping 2000 people who have lost limbs walk again with the help of artificial legs and arms. Donaldson says, "My biggest goal in life is to make a lot of money and then before I die give it away."

Jimmy Donaldson is great at what he does because he cares about the little things. When he gives advice to people trying to have success on YouTube, he says, they should pay attention to the topic, title, and thumbnail. Paying attention to all three and trying hard to make sure the content would be interesting to viewers is how to find success, according to Donaldson. He wants to do his absolute best. As he says, "Literally all I do every single hour of every day is obsess over how I can make the best videos possible."

Paying attention to details can be boring and tiring, but it can lead to great success in many areas of life.

What small things could you do every day to become better at something you like?

Think about your favorite activity (like a sport or a game). How often do you try your hardest when doing it?

What might help you try your best more often, even when things are hard?

THE MAN WHO SHOWED NO FEAR

They walked toward the tiny aircraft, the African sun beating down.

"How long do you think this flight will take?" the tall, dark-skinned man asked his companion.

"Not long, Madiba," Richard answered. "It's just a quick trip."

"It's a shame," Madiba said with a face-splitting smile, holding up his folded copy of The Bantu World. "I had hoped to finish the whole paper before we landed."

Together they climbed the steps and found their seats.

As he sat, Richard shook his head. "You're the only person I know who reads every stupid story in the newspaper. You act like it's all interesting and exciting."

Madiba frowned. "It is, Richard. All the years I spent in prison, I never once held a newspaper in my hand. In fact, when I was on Robben Island, I was put in solitary confinement several times for having little clippings that people snuck to me. Reading about what is happening in our world is a precious gift. I was denied it for many years. Now I intend to enjoy reading every word of it for as long as these old eyes let me."

And with that, Madiba settled into his seat and began reading, only stopping to greet the other two passengers when they boarded.

As they rose into the air, Richard chatted with his companions. Madiba read, and they left him to his quiet luxury. The plane traveled on without a hitch.

Until it didn't.

"Richard," Madiba said, and Richard turned to him. The man's long, brown finger pointed out the window to the plane's stationary propeller. It just sat there. Motionless. While they soared thousands of feet above the earth.

Richard's voice caught in his throat.

Madiba was the picture of calmness. "Richard, you might want to inform the pilot that the propeller isn't working," he said, his voice not even strained.

"Yes, Madiba," Richard croaked, standing and making his way to the cockpit. "Excuse me, sir," he said.

The pilot, looking flustered, turned to face him, "Yes, what?"

"We just wanted to tell you," Richard's voice cracked, and he cleared his throat. "We just wanted to tell you that the propeller on the left side of the plane doesn't...doesn't seem to be working."

"Yes, I know," the pilot said. "I'm a pilot. You don't think I notice when a propeller quits? Go back and sit down. We've called the airport. They have the ambulances out there, and they're going to coat the runway with foam or whatever they do."

Richard nodded. "Yes. Of course. Thank you very much, sir. Sorry to bother you." Trying to keep his breathing slow, he edged his way back to his seat. He told Madiba what the pilot had said.

The man nodded his head. "Yes." Then, he raised his newspaper and continued reading.

Richard gripped his armrests, barely restraining his panic. He fixed his eyes on Madiba, reading without a care. Good heavens, wasn't the man scared at all? Perhaps after so much time in prison, death held no fear anymore.

As the plane descended and they headed toward the runway, Richard watched Madiba turn the pages of his newspaper. When their wheels hit the ground, Richard felt the muscles in his shoulders relax. They were safe. It wasn't until the plane stopped and the door opened that Madiba lowered his paper and tucked it under his arm. He rose and followed Richard off the plane.

As they headed into the airport, Madiba turned to Richard, that smile splitting his face once again. "Man, I was scared up there," he said.

Richard stared at him, stunned. Madiba had not looked afraid. He had been totally in control, not the smallest trace of fear in his face, in his voice, or in his manner. He'd hidden it completely the entire time.

Nelson Mandela, sometimes known by his clan name, Madiba, lived fearlessly throughout his life. When Mandela was a young man, in 1948, his native land, South Africa, entered an oppressive political regime called apartheid. This regime was essentially legalized racism in which whites, the smallest racial group in South Africa at the time, were given power and privileges that were denied to the the Black people living there.

Mandela soon began fighting apartheid through different organizations, including the African National Congress. Mandela spoke out against this racist system. Defying the system could lead to losing one's job, facing physical abuse from the police, imprisonment, and even death.

Though Mandela knew about all these risks, he continued to fight against apartheid. He was eventually tried for sabotaging and attempting to violently overthrow the government. The court found him guilty and sentenced him to life in prison.

Though prison was a horrible experience for Mandela, he didn't give in to fear while there. He continued to dedicate himself to fighting the government even while behind bars. He studied to gain his law degree. He wrote letters and an autobiography that he smuggled out. Near the end of his time in prison, political leaders offered Mandela his freedom if he would admit that certain things he said weren't true. Mandela refused. He was not afraid to serve more time in prison if it meant that his country might be freed from its corrupt and racist policies.

Mandela was eventually released and apartheid was abolished. He continued to work for a government where all the people of South Africa were fairly represented. In 1994, South Africa held its first representative election. Mandela became the first democratically elected president of his country. He continued to serve his people, promoting justice, peace, and reconciliation, for the rest of his life.

Richard Stengl wrote of this incident on the airplane with Mandela. He said it showed him what made Mandela such an incredible leader. After watching Madiba hide his fear so completely, "It was such a revelation because that's what courage is. Courage is not, not being scared. Courage is being terrified and not showing it. So I was enheartened.

I was given courage by looking at him, because he was pretending not to be scared, and that's what he did for his whole life. The more you pretend that you're not scared, the more not scared you become. The more you inhabit that role."

Mandela overcame fear of being imprisoned, of being harmed, of losing everyone and everything. He overcame it for the benefit of his people. He overcame it because he knew there was something more important than his own safety. It was the betterment of his people and his society.

The world would be a better place if we all looked around and asked ourselves, "What could I do to improve this planet?" Changes happen, little by little, as each individual does what they can to bring about that change. How do you want to see the world changed? What's something you can do about it?

I'VE JUST GOT TO PLAY

"How bad is it, Doctor?" the father asked while his son, Leo, lay on the hospital bed, groaning, a cold pack on his face.

The doctor put up the x-ray. "It's a fracture to the cheekbone."

"A fracture?"

"That's just a medical term for a broken bone," the doctor said. "This is a pretty good one. What did you say he hit?"

"Another player's elbow," his father said.

"Ah yes, elbows. The injury all-stars of the sports world. Well, we'll set the bone, and it should be healed up again in about six weeks."

The father's eyebrows shot up. "Six weeks?"

"Yes, that ought to do it," the doctor said, peering at the x-ray again.

"But my son is in a football tournament. The final game is only eight days away."

"Oh sir, I'm sorry, but your son won't be able to play in eight days."

Leo's voice sounded from the bed, and they turned to see him sitting up. "I can't miss the game!"

"Leo, I don't think you should be sitting up right now," his father said. "They haven't even set your bone."

"I'm fine," the boy said. "I'll be fine. I've got to play that game."

"Sir, that is impossible," the doctor said to the father. "I think you're probably aware that the skull protects the brain as well as the eyes. Your son cannot play a contact sport eight days after he's broken part of his skull. If anything jars the bone while it isn't securely mended, it could cause much worse damage." He turned to the boy. "I'm sorry, son, but you'll have to sit this one out."

As they left the hospital, Leo turned to his father. "I have to play," he said.

"You heard what the doctor said."

"I'll be fine. But I can't miss the game. It's the most important one of the season!"

His father sighed. "We'll talk to your coach, but Leo, you really shouldn't."

"I have to."

After conferring with the coach, Leo and his father found out another player had suffered a similar injury at the beginning of the season.

A face mask specialist had made him a protective mask to cover the damaged bone. After much discussion, they decided Leo could play.

"But only," his coach told him, "if you wear the mask the entire time. And you still need to be careful."

"Don't worry," Leo said. "I'll be fine. Just so I get to play."

Leo wore the mask for practice. When Coach Garcia asked him how he was, he said, "Honestly boss, there's no problem."

And then it was time for the final. Leo assumed his starting position wearing his mask like he was supposed to. Everything went fine. For seven minutes.

After that, Leo jogged over to the bench and threw down the mask.

"I can't see," he told his coach. "It's making me sweat too much."

Coach Garcia jumped his feet. "No way, Leo! It's not safe!"

"Just give me 20 minutes, Coach," Leo called back as he jogged to his position. "Then you can replace me."

Leo scored two goals in those twenty minutes, and his face remained intact.

He trotted off the field obediently when his time was up. His father had come to the bench to meet him. He hugged his son.

"Boy, that was amazing, but I was terrified the whole time."

"You don't have to worry about me," Leo said. "I'm fine. I've just got to play."

Lionel "Leo" Messi is thought by many to be the greatest football (soccer) player of all time. Messi loved football from the very beginning. For the Messis, soccer was a family activity. Leo constantly played with his brothers and cousins. His grandmother took him to practices and games, and his father coached him when he was four.

When Leo was six, he joined a soccer club and played for about 6 years, scoring nearly 500 goals. He was good.

But at 10 years old, Messi faced a significant challenge in his football career. He had a condition where his body didn't produce enough growth hormone, stunting his growth and causing other health issues. The issue was treatable, but the treatment cost too much for his family to afford.

Leo could have given up and said that his career as a professional football player wasn't meant to be. However, he and his family didn't. They looked for help from soccer teams. At age 13, Leo joined the Barcelona team, which began to pay for his treatments.

Messi has since become a football legend. He's scored more goals than anyone else in the professional men's Spanish league, than anyone else who's ever played on his Barcelona team, on any South American national team, and in the 21st century.

Though Leo has had great success, it hasn't come without difficulty. His broken cheekbone hasn't been his only injury. He's suffered muscle tears in his thighs, hamstrings, and calves. He's broken bones. There's hardly been a year in his professional career that he hasn't been injured in some way. Yet, he keeps playing. He keeps at it because he loves soccer too much to stop. He's willing to face pain and difficulty because, to him, it's worth it.

As Messi says, "I always thought I wanted to play professionally, and I always knew that to do that I'd have to make a lot of sacrifices. I made sacrifices by leaving Argentina, leaving my family to start a new life. I changed my friends, my people. Everything. But everything I did, I did for football, to achieve my dream."

Messi gave and still gives up a lot for his football career. Usually we have to make sacrifices to do our absolute best at something. We have to figure out what's truly important to us and make it a priority. Have you ever made a sacrifice for someone or something you love? What kinds of things might you have to sacrifice to be really good at something?

YOU'VE GOT TO START SOMEWHERE

Stanley sighed as he waited at the sandwich counter. He was the lucky guy who got to pick up lunch for his coworkers. How glamorous his job was.

Stanley had dreamed of being a big-time writer for as long as he could remember. He wasn't bad either. He'd won "The Biggest News of the Week Contest" three weeks in a row in the New York Herald Tribune. The editor had told him he ought to think about becoming a writer.

A writer. Stanley loved writing. Maybe he could write some book as famous as The Good Earth or Gone With the Wind or The Scarlet Pimpernel. He'd written obituaries and press releases before. But what if he could write something really great? Something his kids and grandkids would have to read in school?

So he'd been really excited when his father told him Martin, his cousin Jean's husband who was an actual publisher, had a position for him. Granted, Martin was only the publisher of Timely Comics. It wasn't serious literature. But still, you had to start somewhere.

But this somewhere wasn't quite what he'd thought. He hadn't written a word since he started this lousy job. He'd filled up inkwells. He'd erased pencil marks on the comic sketches. He'd proofread. Oh, and he got to be the pickup guy for lunch.

"Order up," the man behind the counter said, and Stanley grabbed the brown bags, nodding at the worker with a feeble thank-you. He slouched back to the office and distributed the orders.

"Mr. Kirby, I've got your sandwich," he said to one of the writers, whose head was bent over his drawing board.

Mr. Kirby didn't look up. "Yeah, thanks Stanley."

Stanley began to walk away.

"Hey kid, hold on a second." Mr. Kirby sat up and looked at him.

"Yes sir?"

"You write, don't you?"

Stanley shrugged. "Not here. I wrote in high school though. Obituaries and press releases and competitions. I know enough that they let me proofread."

Mr. Kirby nodded. "Okay, listen. We've got a couple of pages we need filled for the next edition. No pictures or any of that. Just straight text. Something that fits in with the superheroes we've been crafting. You know the stories, right?"

"Yeah, I know. I've seen most of them while proofreading, erasing, or just looking over you guys' shoulders."

Mr. Kirby smiled. "Then you're perfect for the job. Two pages. You make up the story. Why don't you write something about Captain America?"

It was Stanley's turn to nod. "Uh, okay sir."

"What's the matter?"

"Well, it's not really the type of writing I usually do," he said, scuffing his foot against the carpet.

"Listen kid, if you wanna be a writer, you've got to learn to write anything. Anything at all. Become a word master. Anything with words, you can put it together, all right?"

Stanley nodded again. "All right."

"I need it by tomorrow. Do you think you can get a draft to me by then."

"Yes sir. I'll start it now."

Stanely sat down at a typewriter to think. Well, he wanted to be a writer. This was his chance. Though really, he didn't have a lot of interest in writing for the funny papers. But hey, you had to start somewhere, didn't you?

Stanley clicked away. He handed his draft to Mr. Kirby that night. The man scanned it and looked up. "Pretty good, kid. At least it's good enough for the story filler I needed. Thanks."

"Of course, sir."

The man gave him a wry grin as he looked back at the sheet. "You've decided you don't want to be associated with us, eh?"

"What, sir?"

"No way your name is actually Stan Lee."

Stanley shrugged. "I'm young, sir. I'll start using my real name once I know I'm writing something really important."

Mr. Kirby chuckled. "Okay kid. Have a good night."

"You too, Mr. Kirby."

Stanley Lieber, known mostly by his pen name Stan Lee, is remembered for being one of the main influencers of Marvel Comics. He started work there when he was just 16 years old, doing mundane tasks like filling up inkwells and picking up lunches.

Lieber wasn't really interested in the comic book industry, instead wanting to write more serious literature.

However, he soon was promoted to more important jobs, first writing filler stories, then actual illustrated stories for the publication. At just 19 years old, they made him an editor. Not wanting to tarnish his name with the fluffy and unimportant comic book industry, he used the pseudonym Stan Lee, thinking he'd start using his real name when he wrote that famous literary novel he had planned.

He wrote for his cousin-in-law's publication for many years, eventually growing sick of the writing industry in general. He was thinking about quitting around the time that his publisher asked him to come up with a new superhero team. Superheroes were gaining popularity in the late 1950s. Lieber's wife told him to write the stories how he liked. The worst they could do was fire him, and he already wanted to quit anyway.

Stanley worked with Jack Kirby, who'd been working for Timely since before he started, to create the Fantastic Four. These superheroes were different than their forebears. They weren't perfect and altruistic. They were flawed, bickered, questioned their identities, and not always sure about how to do the right thing.

They made mistakes and had flaws. Lieber had taken literary themes about humanity and brought them into the world of comics. Around the same time, Timely Comics began rebranding itself as Marvel Comics.

Lieber eventually attained immense fame and success, having had a hand in the beginnings of a hugely successful franchise. He's credited with co-creating famous characters like The Hulk, Iron Man, The X-Men, and Spiderman.

Stanley didn't feel bad about being a comic book writer in the end. As he said, "I used to be embarrassed because I was just a comic book writer while other people were building bridges or going on to medical careers. And then I began to realize that entertainment is one of the most important things in people's lives. Without it, they might go off the deep end."

Lieber learned to find meaning and importance in his craft. Even though he didn't think it was very respectable in the beginning, he started somewhere, and from that start has come incredible success. What dreams do you have?

Are there ways you could start working on them now, even if those ways are small? What would that look like for you?

TEACHABLE

The door opened and the nine-year-old and his mom kicked off their shoes and headed for the couch. She plopped down while he grabbed the remote and handed it to her.

"Thank you, baby," she said, kissing his temple. She found a channel they both liked, and they settled back together, his head resting on her shoulder.

"You did real good tonight," she said.

"Thanks Mama." He kept his face toward the screen.

"Where did you learn to be so good at football?"

"I don't know. It's just really fun. And Coach Walker teaches us a lot."

"Mmm-hmm. You like Coach Walker, don't you?"

"Yeah, he's nice."

"Coach Walker was talking to me tonight. He was worried about how much you've been missing school and practice."

LeBron sighed. "Yeah, it's hard. But I'm doing okay even so, right Mama?"

She bit her lips and closed her eyes, silent for a moment. "I think you're doing okay, baby. I think you're doing real well for how hard things have been for you. But baby, I want you to be doing better than just okay."

He took his eyes from the screen to look at her. "What do you mean?"

She took a deep breath. "Coach Walker said tonight that, if you wanted to, you could come and stay with his family for a while."

LeBron blinked several times. "Me go and stay with them? But I already stay with you, Mama. What about you?"

She smiled and shrugged. "You know me, baby. I'll be fine. Mama's always fine."

"But you want me to be better than fine. What about you? Don't you deserve to be better than fine too?"

"It's not always about what we deserve, baby. It's about what we can do. And I think this would be a really good chance for you. You've missed so much school and practice, and I know that's because I'm not always around to make sure you're where you need to be. I'm out working or looking for work or looking for a new apartment, and you, baby, you're slipping through the cracks. And you're amazing. You're doing so well with just the little tiny bit I can do for you right now, but just think. What could you be if you went to school every day? If you didn't miss any practices? What could you be if you weren't worried about moving again or starting at a new school? What could you be if you were in one place with good people who could make sure you were where you needed to be all the time? What could you be then, baby?"

Tears streamed down the boy's face. "But Mama, I don't wanna leave you."

She hugged him, and then they were both crying. "I know, baby. I know. I don't want you to leave either." She took another deep breath and held him out from her, wiping the tears from both their cheeks. "But it's not like we'll never see each other. Maybe you could come see me on weekends. And I'll come to your games when I can. And it's only for a little while. Until your mama has a good, stable job and can take care of you right. Only until then."

The boy sniffed.

"Can we just try it, baby? Just for a little while? I really think it would be good for you."

He nodded. "Okay Mama. If it's what you want."

She pulled him in for a hug again. "All I want, baby, is what's best for you." She kissed the top of his head.

The boy moved in with his coach's family. In that house, he learned schedules and routines. He learned how to get up early and wash up quickly in the one bathroom shared by six people. He learned to do his homework as soon as he got home from school. He didn't cause the Walkers any trouble, keeping his space neat, following the rules, and happily eating whatever he was given. He was ready to learn, and he learned quickly that he loved schedules and discipline.

He moved back in with his mom two years later when she had stable work and housing, but he never forgot what he learned while living with the Walkers.

He kept playing sports, and had Dru Joyce II as his basketball coach in a community center league. The boy was the best scorer on his team. One day while driving home, Coach Dru told him, "Bron, if you pass the ball, everyone is going to want to play with you," LeBron heard what he said, and he took it to heart. His coach never had to tell him to pass again.

LeBron James went on to play football and basketball at St. Vincent-St. Mary High School, quickly gaining a national reputation. When football broke his wrist during his junior year, he focused solely on basketball.

The Fighting Irish basketball team won three state championships and one national championship with LeBron on their team. He was the Gatorade National Player of the year twice, the USA Today boys' high school basketball Player of the Year twice, and the Parade High School basketball Player of the Year twice with a slew of other achievements. LeBron didn't go to college, jumping straight into the NBA.

James played for the Cleveland Caveliers for seven years, the Miami Heat for four years, and has been playing for the Los Angeles Lakers since 2018. He has been an NBA champion four times, the NBA Finals MVP 4 times, the NBA MVP 4 times, and an NBA All-Star 20 times. He has scored more points in the NBA than any other player in history, and some argue that he is the greatest player of all time.

James's accomplishments are incredible, and there's no doubt he has a great deal of natural talent. But he never would have excelled to this extent if he hadn't, from the beginning, been ready to learn. James didn't pout about living with the Walkers. He thrived in that home because he wanted to learn what they had to teach. He started passing when his coach told him to pass. And James still listens to critiques, saying, "I like criticism. It makes you strong."

Looking for ways to improve and listening to the advice of those around us brings wisdom. If we're too prideful to listen, if we think we have all the answers, we're missing out on the opportunity to reach our full potential. Wise people look for opportunities to learn and grow. Maybe he'll never be as famous as LeBron, but a teachable person will go a lot farther than a person whose ears are closed.

MAKE THE MOST OF IT

The autumn winds blew through the trees in the chilly garden, but Isaac barely noticed. He scribbled away at his papers as usual, filling them with numbers and figures unintelligible to an average person. Isaac wrote in a flurry and then cried out, "Blast it all!" and threw his pen away.

He'd been stuck here at Woolsthorpe for weeks now. He'd just finished his undergraduate work at Cambridge and been looking forward to getting into really advanced subjects. His mother hadn't even wanted him to go to college. She thought he ought to be a farmer, had set her heart on it, but Isaac couldn't stand working with his hands. His mind longed to learn and be stretched and tested with questions and problems.

But how was he supposed to learn here? By himself? He was supposed to be a student, but he had no teachers other than these books. No one to talk to about what he was learning. No one to help him test out his ideas.

His grandmother was very kind, but she didn't care a fig about mathematics. If Isaac tried to explain what he was studying, she would smile blandly at him and say, "That's nice dear."

Indeed, this had happened half an hour ago. She'd said, "That's very nice, dear. Would you like a cup of tea? You're very pale, you know. You ought to go outside more instead of burying your head in those books all the time."

Well, Isaac had listened to her. He'd gone out to sit in the garden, to try to study. But he felt defeated. How could he do anything worthwhile on his own? Here? At Woolsthorpe?

Isaac stared into the distance. The view was beautiful, but Isaac barely ever noticed. His thoughts were often on what he couldn't see. He wondered if it were foolish for him to ignore the natural world so much to study the mechanisms behind it. After all, the rolling hills and the tree-spotted countryside were breathtaking when you took the time to look.

He stared at a large apple tree, twisting twisting toward the sky. It was picturesque in its stretch toward the heavens. It seemed like it didn't care that it was rooted to the ground. It would stretch as high as it could anyway.

A gust of wind swept into the garden and shook the tree branches. An apple dropped to the ground.

Newton stared at it. It dropped. That was what things always did. When they weren't supported, they moved toward the earth. How peculiar. Why did they do that?

He stood and walked toward the fallen apple. Why didn't they just float up into the sky? Or go sideways? Why always straight toward the earth?

He reached the fruit and picked it up, seeing the bruise on its belly from its fall. He dropped it again. Of course, it fell to the earth once more. He did this over and over until the apple was a pulpy mess. He left it there, going inside to wash the juice off in the basin.

His mind was whirring with questions. Why did everything fall toward the earth? Was it, perhaps, pulled? And if the earth pulls things toward itself, did other heavenly bodies do this as well? It had given him something to study, by George.

"Well, you didn't stay outside very long," his grandmother said with her hands on her hips.

He dried his hands and smiled at her cheerily.

"No, not so long. But it was an excellent idea, going outside. I must do it again soon. Sometimes a change of view does a man all the good in the world."

He kissed her cheek and headed back up to his bedroom to bury himself in his books.

Sir Isaac Newton is one of the most influential mathematicians, physicists, and astronomers in history. He is partly credited with developing calculus, and he made significant advancements in the study of optics. Newton founded the laws of motion and gravitation, which ruled the study of physical science for centuries.

He's the one who finally convinced the scientific community as a whole that the sun did not revolve around the Earth.

Einstein thought he was great. When Einstein's theory of relativity superseded some of Newton's theories, Einstein was apologetic. "Newton, forgive me, you found the only way which in your age was just barely possible for a man with the highest powers of thought and creativity. The concepts which you created are guiding our thinking in physics even today..."

Newton didn't have an easy start to life. His father died three months before he was born, and he came into the world prematurely on Christmas day in 1642. His mother said he was small enough to fit inside a quart mug. She married his step-father when he was three and left him with his grandmother to go and live with her new husband. Newton didn't get along well with either parent.

Newton went to school and, unsurprisingly, became a top student. He went on to study at Cambridge, where he didn't stand out from the crowd too much. Right after he received his bachelor's degree, the university closed because of the spread of the bubonic plague. Newton returned to the home where he'd been born, Woolsthorpe. He remained there for two years.

Many students would take the opportunity to rest from their studies if their school got shut down. Not Newton. He spent his two years at Woolsthorpe studying and developing his ideas. It was at Woolsthorpe where he said he saw the famous apple fall from the tree and began to create his theories of gravitation. He didn't waste his time or wish away difficult circumstances. He made the most of his time, no matter where he was.

Newton lived a long, productive life. His legacy remains. He was a man who threw himself into whatever he was doing with enthusiasm. He didn't let difficulty slow him down. He made the most of every opportunity. He saw life as a mysterious depth to be searched. After all his accomplishments, his remark on himself was this:

"I do not know what I may appear to the world, but to myself I seem to have been only like a boy playing on the sea-shore, and diverting myself in now and then finding a smoother pebble or a prettier shell than ordinary, whilst the great ocean of truth lay all undiscovered before me."

— Isaac Newton

What do you think you could find in the great ocean of truth if you started looking?

THOSE WHO GET BACK ON THEIR FEET

Bear turned on the tap and splashed his face. He turned it off and looked at himself in the mirror. His face looked fine. It always looked fine. The boy was always careful to avoid hitting his face. If Bear looked banged up, teachers might ask him what was wrong. No, the bully was careful to leave marks where they wouldn't show.

Bear dried his hands and pulled up his shirt. He looked at the red marks and wondered if they were bad enough to become bruises this time. He sighed. How much longer would he have to put up with this? He was so tired of being afraid.

He didn't know why that enormous hunk of teenager decided to pick on him specifically. After all, weren't there lots of skinny 13-year-olds at Eaton? But for some reason, he'd become the target. When classes were over, when everyone was out roaming the grounds, the bullies kept finding him. He had the marks to prove it.

Bear sighed. What could he do about this? He didn't want to put up with it until the bully left school. And he didn't want to walk around being afraid either. He didn't want to hide. But what could he do? The boy was five years older than him and so much bigger. How could he ever defend himself?

He walked slowly back to his dormitory, looking around to be sure the coast was clear. Everyone else was out enjoying one of the last warm, sunny days they'd have this fall. He sighed again.

On his way into the dorm, he passed the notice board. Having no desire to face the homework waiting in his room, he dawdled a moment to read it. And there it was. A flier for a karate club. Sundays at 7 PM.

Karate. That sounded cool. And hey, if he learned it, maybe he could learn to stand up to the bully, at least a little. Beginner defensive skills had to be more helpful than no defensive skills. It was something.

Bear told a few of his friends about the club, and they all decided to go together. After dinner one Sunday evening, they strolled over to the gym together. The teacher welcomed them as they entered, and asked them to remove their shoes.

Bear was surprised at the number of kids there. Many were already busy, practicing kicks and punches, sparring with each other. It looked awesome. He couldn't wait to get started.

That was until he did get started. The next two hours were some of the most grueling he'd ever faced in his life. He did push-ups and sit-ups. He learned to form a fist and throw a punch. He stretched. He kicked. He repeated motions again and again and again until his muscles screamed at him to stop. He was not as good as his friends, being somewhat weaker and less flexible than they were, but he did his best.

At the end of the night, they trudged back to the dorm, exhausted.

"Well, I'm never doing that again," his friend John said.

"Really?" Bear asked.

"Of course not!" John said. "That was murder, mate! And it was only the first class. Things only get harder from here."

"I think I'll try it again next week," Bertrand said, then laughed. "If I can walk normally again by then."

"I know I'm going back," Bear said. "I think it's so cool what the sensei said about karate being about guile over power and technique over force. It's awesome how you can be good at it no matter how small you are."

"Yeah, sure," said John with a shrug. They headed back up to their rooms.

Bear did stick with karate. The friends who'd signed up with him slowly disappeared as the weeks passed, but he kept going. He got stronger and fitter. A few years later, he earned his black belt. Somewhere along the way, the bullying stopped. But Bear wasn't doing karate to ward off enemies anymore. He was now doing it because he loved it.

Bear Grylls is largely known as a TV personality. He's starred in survival shows like Worst-Case Scenario, Get Out Alive, and is most well-known for Man vs. Wild. He is famous for accomplishing amazing/disgusting physical feats and showing viewers survival techniques in incredibly hostile environments. Some of these experiences include swimming naked across an arctic river, using vines to climb down cliffs, and getting liquid in the desert by squeezing it into his mouth from fresh elephant dung.

One of Bear's most marked qualities is his perseverance. He never quits. He does what's necessary to survive, no matter how hard it is. He doesn't shy away from hardship, and he keeps going no matter what.

This is a quality he learned in his youth in a few different ways. He was in the Scouts as a kid, and also, in his early teens, he took up karate to help him defend himself from bullies. He learned discipline and focus as well as survival skills. He learned determination.

Now Grylls is the Chief Scout of the Scout Association in the United Kingdom, and he tries to pass on his determination to young people. As Bear puts it, "The rewards in life don't always go to the biggest or the bravest, the cleverest, or even the best. The rewards in life go to the dogged and the determined, to the tenacious, those who get back on their feet when they get kicked."

Bear wasn't always brave and determined. When he was bullied at school, he was just plain scared. However, he looked for a solution to his bullying problem, and through this solution, he learned the power of determination. When have you had to practice determination in your life? What skills could you improve if you used determination to get better at them?

CONCLUSION

You've just finished reading about men, all different, all great. These guys had a lot in common. Most had strong work ethics. Most showed perseverance. Most viewed failure and mistakes not as reasons to quit, but as opportunities to learn. They had ingenuity and creativity. They valued the knowledge they had and sought to gain more.

But the main thing that knits these men together is the fact that they are, in fact, men. They started out as children, just like you. Some came from stable families and homes, some did not. Some were expected to make the most of their lives from the get-go, others were not. Any could have given up on their path to success, said all of it was too hard or that they'd rather pursue excellence in moderation. They could have settled for normal, status-quo lives. This is, in fact, what most people do.

But the fact remains that heroes are made, not born. Many of these men were told they would fail, that they didn't have what it took, that they ought to settle for good enough. But good wasn't enough for them. They desired greatness, for humanity, for the world, and for themselves. They refused to settle for less.

Now the same choice is before you. Will you seek to make something great of your life? Will you choose to be fearless like Nelson Mandela and Neil Armstrong? Will you choose to be innovative like Ben Franklin? Will you choose to be empathetic like Barack Obama and Patch Adams? Will you choose to be a learner like LeBron and Alan Turing? Will you choose to make the best of things like Isaac Newton and Stan Lee? Will you choose to pursue excellence like MrBeast and Tony Hawk? Will you choose to dream big like the Rock? Will you choose to learn discipline like Usain Bolt? Will you choose to keep going no matter what like Leo Messi and Bear Grylls?

Many people look at the success of others and attribute it to privilege or being born with special talents or intellectual capacity. There's no doubt that some people have an easier time climbing the ladder of success than others. But many of these men did not have an easy time. In the end, a person's choices have far more impact on who they are than their privilege and their talents.

So now, the question lies with you. Who will you choose to be? What will you make of your life?

Because no one else will make it for you. You will always be the one who has to decide. You have what you've been given, just like each of the men with this book. They chose to use it for greatness.

What will you do with what you've got?

We'd love to hear what you think. If these stories inspired you or made you realize that the possibilities in your life are endless, let us know! It only takes a few seconds and can be just a couple of words.
As a family-run business, each review helps us create more stories for young dreamers like you.

So, grab your phone, scan that QR code, and who knows—maybe one day I'll be writing a story about your amazing life!

CLAIM YOUR FREE GIFT!

Your adventure continues... Scan the QR code
or go to: www.tinyurl.com/2mj9vhn3 for instant access to
our special story collection!

GET IT HERE!

Made in the USA
Monee, IL
27 October 2024

68724965R00046